🐾 A GOLDEN BOOK • NEW YORK

T#: 471867
ISBN 978-0-399-55358-5
randomhousekids.com
MANUFACTURED IN CHINA
10 9 8 7 6 5 4 3 2

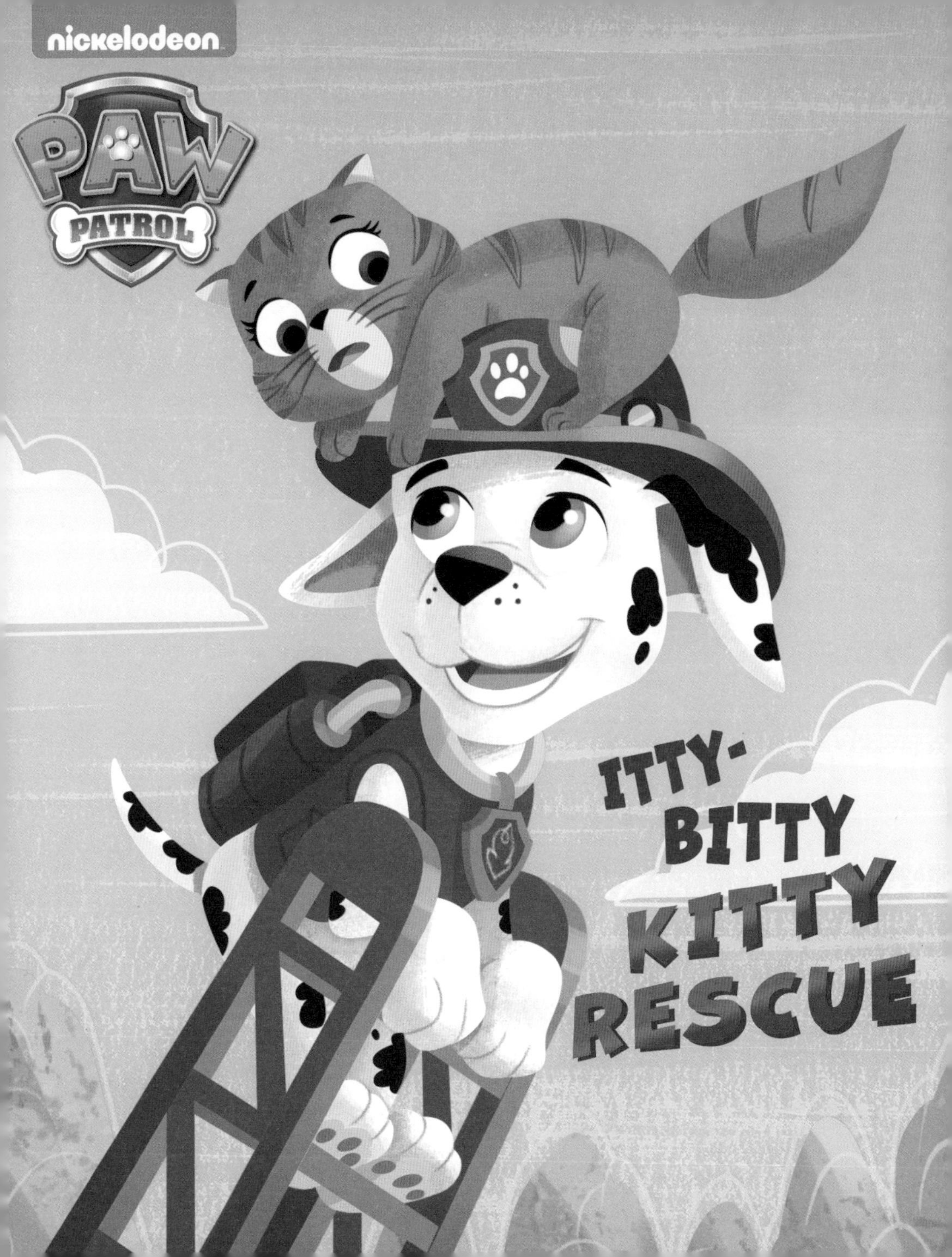
nickelodeon
PAW PATROL
ITTY-BITTY KITTY RESCUE

It was a warm, sunny day. Chase and Rubble were having a great time playing catch at the beach. Then they heard a far-off cry.

"*Meow! Meow!*"

A kitten was clinging to a toy boat out in the water!

"Uh-oh!" Rubble exclaimed. "That little kitty is in trouble."

"We need to tell Ryder," Chase said.

Chase and Rubble raced to the Lookout to tell Ryder about the kitty.

"No job is too big, no pup is too small!" declared Ryder. He pushed a button on his PupPad and sounded the PAW Patrol Alarm.

Minutes later, Marshall, Skye, Rocky, and Zuma joined their puppy pals at the Lookout.

"PAW Patrol is ready for action," reported Chase, sitting at attention.

"A kitten is floating out to sea," Ryder announced, pointing to the viewing screen behind him.

"We have to save the itty-bitty kitty!" exclaimed Rubble. Then he straightened up and added, "I mean, ahem, we have to save the kitten."

"Zuma, your hovercraft is perfect for a water rescue," Ryder said.

"Ready, set, get wet!" Zuma barked.

"And, Skye," Ryder continued, "I'll need you and your helicopter to help find the kitten quickly."

"This pup's got to fly!" Skye exclaimed.

Zuma's hovercraft splashed across Adventure Bay. Ryder turned his ATV into a Jet Ski and followed. Up above, Sky zoomed through the air. She quickly spotted the kitten.

"We're here to help you," Ryder said, easing his Jet Ski to a stop.

The little kitten jumped from her boat and landed on Zuma's head. The startled pup fell into the water.

Zuma yelled, "Don't touch the—"

The kitten accidentally hit the throttle and raced off on the hovercraft.

The hovercraft zoomed around the bay. Overhead, Skye turned this way and that, trying to follow the hovercraft's twisting course.

"This kitty is making me dizzy," she groaned.

Ryder pulled up next to the hovercraft and jumped on board. He stopped the engine and gently picked up the shivering kitten.

"Everything's all right," he said, pulling a slimy piece of seaweed off the kitten. "Let's take you back to dry land and get you cleaned up."

Later that day, Rubble skateboarded into Katie's Pet Parlor with his new BFF. "Aww, whose cute kitty is that?" Katie asked. "We don't know," Rubble explained. "We found her on the bay with no collar or tags, just this purple ribbon."

"Does the kitty-widdy want a nice warm bath?" Rubble asked.

"*Meow*," the kitten replied.

"Do you want me to do it?" Katie asked. "Cats can be a little tricky to bathe."

"Tricky?" Rubble said. "Not this little sweetie."

But the kitten had other ideas. The moment she touched the water, she jumped away with a screech.

She scurried along shelves, knocking over bottles of shampoo.

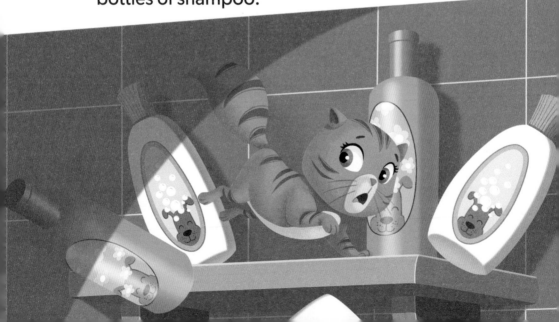

Rubble slipped on a spinning bottle.

The kitten fell onto Rubble's skateboard
and rolled out the door!

Down the street from Katie's Pet Parlor, Ryder got a message from Rocky: *"A little girl is looking for her lost kitty named Precious."*

Ryder recognized the kitten in the picture the girl was holding. Before he could say a word, Precious rolled past on Rubble's skateboard. She skated down a hill and disappeared into town.

"Chase, it's time to use your Super Sniffer!"
Ryder said.

Chase needed something with the kitty's scent
on it. Luckily, they had her purple ribbon.

Chase took a deep sniff. "She went that way—
ACHOO! Sorry. Cat hair makes me sneeze."

Sniff, sniff, sniff.

Chase followed the scent until he found Rubble's skateboard at the bottom of the town hall steps.

"Good sniffing," Ryder said.

Ryder and the pups looked around and saw a shocking sight.

The kitty was inside the town hall bell tower!

Ryder pulled out his PupPad and called for Marshall and his fire truck.

"I'm all fired up!" Marshall said as his fire truck screeched to a halt in front of the town hall. He arrived at the same time as the kitty's owner.

Ryder told Marshall to put up his ladder. "We need to get the kitten down from that tower."

"I'm on it," Marshall declared. He extended the truck's ladder and carefully started to climb.

Marshall reached the top of the ladder. The scared little kitten was clinging desperately to a rope in the tower.

"I'll get you down safely," Marshall said. "Come here."

"*Meow,*" Precious whimpered.

The kitten jumped from the rope. She tried to grab Marshall's helmet but missed—and clutched his face instead.

"Whoa!" Marshall yelped. He couldn't see!

The ladder shook. Marshall lost his grip. He and the kitten fell off the ladder!

Ryder caught Marshall, and the little kitty tumbled into her owner's arms.

"Precious!" the girl exclaimed. "You're okay! You owe these brave pups a thank-you for all their help."

"Whenever you need us," Ryder said, "just yelp for help!"

nickelodeon

PAW PATROL

PUPPY BIRTHDAY TO YOU!

One windy afternoon in Adventure Bay, a box moved down the street toward Katie's Pet Parlor. But this box wasn't being blown by the wind. *It was creeping down the street on eight paws!*

Suddenly, a big gust blew the box away, revealing Skye and Rubble underneath. They quickly scampered into the shop.

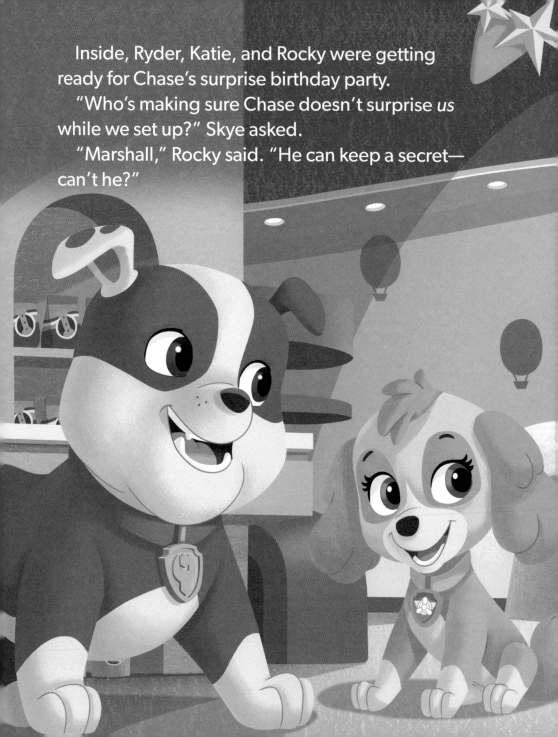

Inside, Ryder, Katie, and Rocky were getting ready for Chase's surprise birthday party.

"Who's making sure Chase doesn't surprise *us* while we set up?" Skye asked.

"Marshall," Rocky said. "He can keep a secret— can't he?"

Across town, Marshall and Chase were playing in Pup Park. They swung on the swings and slid down the slide.

"Maybe we should go find Ryder and the pups," Chase said.

"No!" Marshall protested. "We can't! Because it's, um, so nice out."

Just then, the wind picked up again and blew them right across the park!

Back at the Pet Parlor, the lights suddenly went dark, and Katie's mixer stopped.

"All the lights on the street are out!" Rocky yelped.

Ryder thought he knew what was wrong. "PAW Patrol, to the Lookout!"

The team raced to the Lookout. But without electricity, the doors wouldn't open. Luckily, Rocky had a screwdriver, which did the trick.

Once they were inside, Ryder used his
telescope to check Adventure Bay's windmills.
"Just as I thought," he said. "The wind broke
a propeller. Since the windmill can't turn, it can't
make electricity. We need to fix it!"

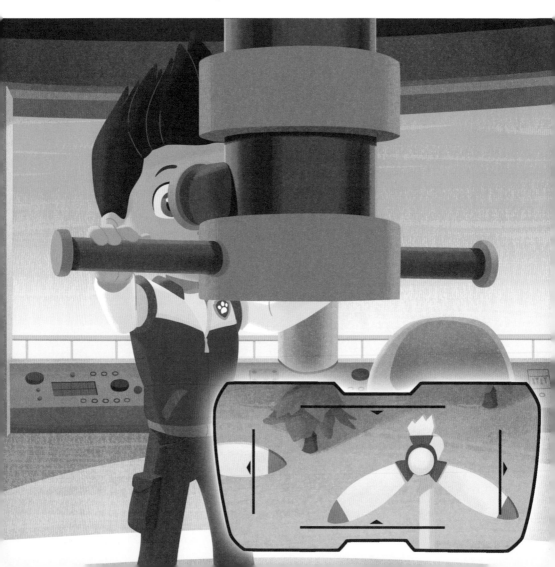

Ryder looked at Rocky. "We'll need something from your truck to fix the broken blade."

"Green means go!" Rocky said, preparing for action.

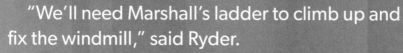

"We'll need Marshall's ladder to climb up and fix the windmill," said Ryder.

Marshall nodded. "I'm fired up!"

"Chase, the traffic lights won't work without electricity," Ryder continued. "I need you to use your siren and megaphone to direct traffic."

"These paws uphold the laws," Chase declared.

Meanwhile, Skye, Zuma, and Rubble raced back to the Pet Parlor to continue setting up for Chase's surprise party. It was very dark, but Katie had a flashlight.

At the center of town, Chase busily directed traffic.
"You're our hero," Mayor Goodway said as she
crossed the street safely.
"I'm just doing my PAW Patrol duty," Chase said.

Up in the hills, Ryder, Marshall, and Rocky went
to work on the broken windmill. Ryder climbed
Marshall's ladder and removed the old blade
while Rocky looked for a replacement piece.

"No, not a tire . . . not a lawn chair," Rocky
said, pulling stuff out of his truck. At last he found
what he wanted. "Here it is—my old surfboard!

"This surfboard will catch a breeze and help turn it into electricity," Rocky said as he bolted the board into place. The wind picked up and the windmill started to turn. Lights came on all over Adventure Bay!

The traffic lights started working again.
"Ryder and the PAW Patrol did it!" Chase
announced through his megaphone. "My work
here is done!"

The lights in the Pet Parlor glowed brightly. "Hooray!" cheered Skye, but then she frowned. "Aw! There's no time to make a cake." Katie thought for a moment. "I have an idea!"

As Chase drove back to the Lookout, he got a call from Ryder. "We need you at Katie's—in a hurry!"

When Chase got there, everything was dark and quiet.

Chase stepped inside. The lights went on. "SURPRISE!" everyone yelled.

Chase was amazed. "Wow! You guys turned the lights back on AND made a party for me?"

"We didn't have time to bake you a real cake," Katie said, "so we hope you like your pup-treat cookie cake."

"Whenever it's your birthday, just yelp
for help!" Ryder said with a laugh.
All the puppies cheered and enjoyed
a taste of Chase's special cake.

PIRATE PUPS!

One day, while exploring the cliffs above Adventure Bay, Cap'n Turbot slipped and fell down a dark hole. At the bottom, he discovered an old pirate hideout.

He was stuck in the creepy cavern, but he knew who could help him: the PAW Patrol!

Ryder called the PAW Patrol to the Lookout and told them about Cap'n Turbot.

"He's stuck in a cavern filled with pirate stuff, and he thinks it might be the hideout of the legendary Captain Blackfur!" Ryder said. "No one knows what he looked like or what happened to his treasure."

Ryder needed Chase and Rubble for the
rescue, but he told the rest of the pups to
be ready, just in case.
　　Rubble was excited. He really wanted
to be a pirate!

Ryder, Chase, and Rubble raced to the cliffs and found the hole.

"Chase," Ryder said, "I need your winch hook to lower me into the cave."

"Chase is on the case!" He pulled the hook over, and Ryder locked it onto his safety belt.

Chase carefully lowered Ryder into the dark hole.

The pups joined Ryder and Cap'n Turbot down below. Using Chase's spotlight, they found cool pirate stuff—a spyglass, a flag, and a real pirate hat! Ryder put the hat on Rubble's head.

"*Arr!*" said Rubble. "Shiver me timbers!"

Chase sniffed the air. "I smell seawater," he said. He followed the scent and discovered a secret passage! But it was blocked by rocks.

"That must be the way to the beach," said Ryder.

"Stand back, landlubbers!" said Rubble as he cleared the way with his digger.

Ryder and the pups followed the passage to a beach. They found an old bottle with part of a map inside it.

"Is it a pirate treasure map?" Rubble asked.

"Could be," said Ryder. "We need all paws on deck to solve this mystery."

Ryder called the rest of the pups to the beach and told them that the map had been torn into three pieces.

"There's a clue to where we'll find the next piece," he said. "*'The part of the map that you seek hides in the big parrot's beak.'*"

The pups thought about the clue. Suddenly,
Rocky said, "Those boulders at the bottom of Jake's
Mountain kind of look like a parrot!"
"Let's check it out," Chase barked.

The team hurried to the rocks that looked like a giant parrot. Skye flew up and found a bottle in its beak. Another piece of the map was inside!

Rocky taped the pieces together, and
Ryder read the next clue: "'*From atop
Parrot Rock, look toward the sea. A clue
hides in the hollow of a very big tree.*'"

"If we can solve that clue," Ryder said, "we should find Blackfur's treasure!"

Chase thought for a moment. "The biggest trees around are in Little Hooty's forest."

"Good thinking!" Ryder exclaimed.

The forest was filled with lots of big trees, so
Chase asked Little Hooty if he had seen an old
bottle in any of the branches. He had!
Little Hooty fluttered up to a hole high in a tree.

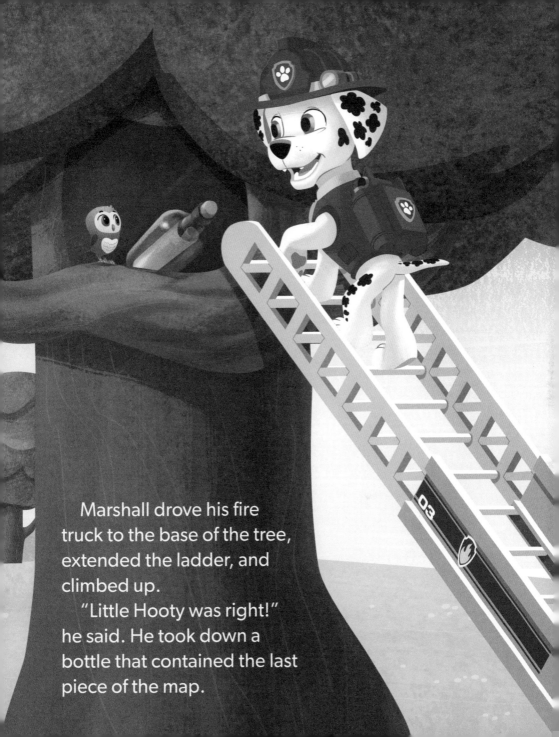

Marshall drove his fire truck to the base of the tree, extended the ladder, and climbed up.

"Little Hooty was right!" he said. He took down a bottle that contained the last piece of the map.

Rocky taped the pieces together. They now had the whole map! Ryder read the final clue: *"'Walk twenty paces from the tree toward setting sun and rising sea.'"*

Ryder turned to face the sun and the sea, and he started walking.

From the edge of the cliff, Ryder and the pups saw something amazing through the fog.

It was an old pirate ship next to a deserted island!

"Do you think it's Captain Blackfur's ship?" Rubble asked.

The PAW Patrol worked together to pull the ship onto the beach.

News of the find spread through Adventure Bay. Mayor Goodway and her pet chicken, Chickaletta, came to see the exciting discovery.

On board, Ryder, Cap'n Turbot, and the pups found an old treasure chest. Inside were coins, jewels, a gold bone, and even a fancy dog bowl.

"Why would a pirate captain have a dog bowl?" Marshall asked.

Then, digging through the treasure, Ryder found an old picture of Captain Blackfur.

Captain Blackfur was a pirate pup!
"He looks just like me, except with a *black fur* beard!" Rubble exclaimed.
The team let out a mighty *"Arr!"*
Three cheers for the pirate pups of the PAW Patrol!